Keep being
Super.
PASTOWWW!!!
Melissa Miles
2020

JEREMIAH JUSTICE

SAVES THE DAY!

by **Melissa Miles**

illustrated by **Rashad Doucet**

Hillcrest Press

Jeremiah Justice discovered his superpower the day he tripped while running through the yard.

Before he knew it, he was soaring through the air!

Just when he thought he was going to crash...

PASHOWWW!!!

A gigantic swirling gust of air blew him back onto his feet.

The blast came from the plastic tube in his neck that helped him breathe.

"Can I make it happen again?" he wondered.

Jeremiah Justice spotted some dandelions in the yard.

He took a deep breath and...

A cloud of fluffy white seeds soared into the
sky and spiraled around him.

He pumped his fist in the air.
He'd done it again!

Jeremiah Justice decided he could be the superhero his city needed. He named his power, "The Super Tornado Blaster!"

Meanwhile... The notorious villain, Mr. Menace, escaped justice again!

Jeremiah Justice practiced his Super Tornado Blaster. There were a few unfortunate mishaps.

PASHOWWW!!
"Oops!"

PASHOWWW!!

"Bow wow!"

While Jeremiah Justice learned to control the Super Tornado Blaster, Mr. Menace continued his crime spree.

People wondered if Mr. Menace could ever be stopped.

"What this city needs is a superhero," said the news anchorwoman.

So, Jeremiah Justice made a superhero suit...
Just in case.

"People will trust a kid in a superhero suit," Jeremiah Justice told his grandma. "More than a kid in shorts and flip-flops."

When the neighbor's cat got stuck in a tree, Jeremiah Justice was excited. "Finally, a chance to test my Super Tornado Blaster!"

Ms. Miller thanked Jeremiah Justice with a plate of warm cookies.

Her cat didn't thank him at all.

One day at recess, Jeremiah Justice spotted Mr. Menace outside the playground fence.

He was picking the lock on the storage building!

The lock opened! Jeremiah Justice knew he had to act fast. Mr. Menace was famously speedy!

Jeremiah Justice sprang into action.

But things didn't go exactly as planned...

But, Mr. Menace didn't know about the Super Tornado Blaster!

He wasn't laughing
for long.

Jeremiah Justice took a
deep breath and...

PASHOWWW!!

Mr. Menace shot into the air...

...and barely missed a helicopter!

When Mr. Menace landed, the police were waiting.

He'd made a big mistake trying to steal from Thunderbolt Elementary School!

His teacher, Ms. Hall shouted, "Jeremiah Justice Saves the Day!"

After that, not many villains dared to commit crimes in his city. But if they did, Jeremiah Justice would be ready...

STAY TUNED FOR MORE
ADVENTURES!

Find out more!

A tracheostomy (track-ee-os-tohmee) is a tiny surgical opening on the neck into the windpipe (trachea). A tube is placed into this opening in order to keep an open airway and allow for effective breathing.

Follow

Facebook
@jjsavestheday

Instagram
@supertornadoblaster

Website
anovelwritingconcept.wordpress.com

Acknowledgements

This book wouldn't have been possible without the help of many people, including everyone who generously backed the Kickstarter campaign. Special thanks to Josh Holley, Rachel Miles, William and Linda Johnston, and Lewis Miles for your collaboration. This book would have never been created without you.

The following people donated at the highest level of the campaign and have earned special acknowledgment: Michael and Samantha Bossak, Peg Wise, Linda Beaufort, Vin and Vita Evangelista, Charlotte Leighty, Joanne Hayes and Wendy Phillips, Laura Althoff, The Loft Ladies, Sandra Edwards, and Michelle and Justin Walter.

Thanks also go out to Deborah Halverson for editing services, and to Kristy Dempsey and Crystal Allen for taking the time to read this book and offer your valuable insights.

About

Melissa Miles is a pediatric nurse and certified K-12 educator who's always loved a good story. Working with children has always been her passion, so it's no surprise she wants to create stories for them.

She lives in the Savannah area with her husband and spoiled dog, and is a mom to two wonderful young adults. Melissa believes special needs kids have always been superheroes. Jeremiah Justice Saves the Day is the first book in what will hopefully become a series of special needs superhero books.

This book was published thanks to a Kickstarter campaign, and the proceeds of every book will be donated to a charitable foundation to support kids with special needs.

Rashad Doucet is a New Orleans (by way of Eunice, and Ville Platte Louisiana) native who's been drawing comics since his grandma gave him a pencil and some paper to keep quiet during church.

He's known for his work with Oni Press on comics like Invader Zim, Rick and Morty, Alabaster Shadows and children's books like the Nadia Series from Heart Head Publishing. He's also worked with DC Comics, Stela Comics, and Devil's Due Digital to name a few.

Rashad's currently a professor of Sequential Art at the Savannah College of Art and Design in Savannah, Georgia where he can often be found listening to 80's power ballads and watching way too much anime.

Hardcover ISBN: 978-0-9912117-3-9
Library of Congress Control Number: 2018958131

CPSIA information can be obtained
at www.ICGtesting.com
Printed in the USA
BVHW021331030419
544433BV00002B/7/P